# TRANSFORMERS
## ROBOTS IN DISGUISE

With special thanks to Anne Marie Ryan

ORCHARD BOOKS
Carmelite House
50 Victoria Embankment
London EC4Y 0DZ

First published by Orchard Books in 2018

A CIP catalogue record for this book is available
from the British Library.

ISBN 978 1 40835 152 9

1 3 5 7 9 10 8 6 4 2

Printed in China

MIX
Paper from
responsible sources
FSC® C104740

Orchard Books
An imprint of Hachette Children's Group
Part of The Watts Publishing Group Limited
An Hachette UK Company
www.hachette.co.uk

# TRANSFORMERS
## ROBOTS IN DISGUISE

# GRIMLOCK'S
# BAD FRIEND

ORCHARD

# ROLL OUT!

BUMBLEBEE

SIDESWIPE

GRIMLOCK

STRONGARM

FIXIT

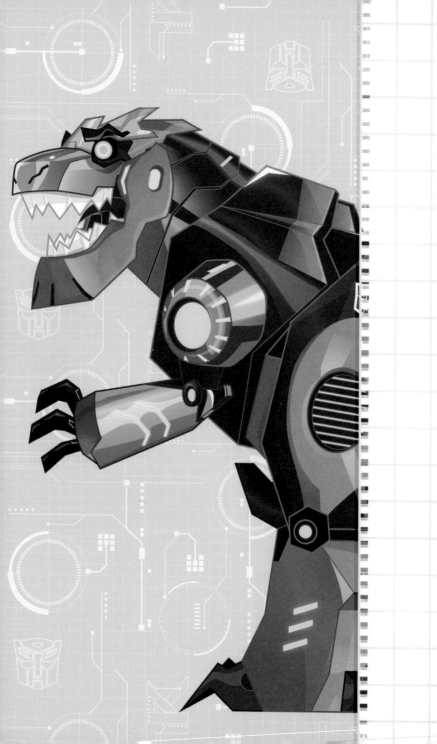

# CONTENTS

# Part One:
# A NEW DINOBOT

# Chapter One

## SOLO PATROL

Grimlock was walking in the woods. He was looking for bad robots called Decepticons. He searched through the trees, but the huge green Dinobot didn't see any bad robots. He didn't see anything interesting at all!

Grimlock called Fixit on his walkie-talkie. Fixit was at the scrapyard. "There are no Decepticons," Grimlock said.

"OK," replied Fixit through the walkie-talkie.

Grimlock punched a tree. "I miss smashing stuff just for fun," he said to himself. "What good is a Dinobot if he's not smashing stuff?"

Grimlock sighed. He felt bored and restless. He really wished there were some bad robots for him to fight.

Suddenly, Grimlock heard a loud noise. He followed the sound and came to an old football field. *SMASH!*

Tall lights tumbled to the ground. *CRASH!*

The scoreboard flew through the air. It nearly hit Grimlock!

Grimlock ran into the arena to find out what was going on.

When the dust settled, he saw something amazing. There was another Dinobot! It was smashing things with its big spiky tail.

Grimlock was very excited to meet another Dinobot.

Grimlock turned into a T-Rex. "That was some cool smashing," he said to the other Dinobot.

"I am called Scowl," said the spiky brown Dinobot. "And I am going to smash this place up. Do you want to help me?" he asked Grimlock.

Grimlock couldn't believe that there was another Dinobot just like him!

## Chapter Two

# A SMASHING TIME

Grimlock looked around at the arena. It was cracked and crumbling. There were diggers and other wrecking machines all around.

"It looks like this place is going to be torn down anyway," said Grimlock. He thought they would be doing the building crew a big favour if he and Scowl knocked the arena down.

"Let's smash!" shouted
Grimlock.

*BASH!* A digger flew across
the arena.

*WHAM!* The stands fell to the
ground with a crash.

*POW!* The snack bar sailed through the air.

Grimlock had lots of fun wrecking the arena. It felt great to be smashing things again!

Soon, the arena was just a pile of dust and rubble.

"That was awesome!" said Grimlock happily. He gave Scowl a tail-five.

"I've got a good idea," said Scowl. "Let's smash up this whole planet together!"

Grimlock turned back into a robot. He showed Scowl his Autobot badge.

"I work with the Autobots," he explained. "We fight any bad Decepticons that want to hurt the people on Earth."

Scowl looked at Grimlock's badge crossly.

"I need to arrest you," Grimlock told Scowl sadly.

## Chapter Three

# GRIMLOCK MAKES A DEAL

Scowl could not believe what he was hearing. Grimlock had been smashing up the arena, too. It was what Dinobots liked to do! Scowl tried to convince Grimlock to change his mind.

"I'm not a bad bot," Scowl told Grimlock. "I just like smashing things."

Grimlock shook his head.

Grimlock was supposed to arrest any Decepticons that he found. They were dangerous!

"Come on, Grim," begged Scowl. "We are practically brothers."

Grimlock felt terrible. He really didn't want to arrest his cool new friend. It was fun to hang out with another Dinobot.

Grimlock thought hard. He decided to make a deal with Scowl. "If I let you go, do you promise not to hurt anyone?" he asked Scowl.

"You mean the little screamers who live on this planet?" Scowl said, laughing.

"Yes. You have to promise not to hurt anyone!" said Grimlock.

"I promise I won't hurt any living thing," Scowl said.

Grimlock trusted Scowl. He let his new friend go.

"Thanks, Grim," said Scowl, turning into a brown robot.

Scowl said goodbye and stomped off through the woods. As Grimlock headed back to the scrapyard, he felt worried. He wasn't sure if he had done the right thing. Would Scowl stick to their deal?

# Part Two:
# TRAIN WRECK

## Chapter Four

# WRECK AND ROLL

When he got back to the scrapyard, Grimlock pretended that everything was fine. He didn't want to tell the other Autobots about meeting Scowl. He knew they would be angry that he hadn't arrested him.

"I didn't see any Decepticons," Grimlock said, crossing his fingers behind his back. "Not even a single one."

Suddenly, Fixit's computer beeped. The little robot had picked up a signal from the woods. "There's a Decepticon near the old arena," Fixit told the Autobots.

"Wasn't that where you were patrolling?" Strongarm asked Grimlock.

Grimlock couldn't lie to his team. Ashamed, he told them that he had seen the other Dinobot, but let him go.

Strongarm was furious. She couldn't believe Grimlock had let a Decepticon go free!

"Scowl said he would not hurt anyone," said Grimlock. "He's a nice guy. He was just smashing stuff. That's just what Dinobots do!"

Fixit searched his database
and discovered that Scowl
worked for Thunderhoof, a
dangerous criminal Decepticon.

Scowl had helped Thunderhoof by destroying lots of people's homes so that Thunderhoof could steal their land.

Grimlock felt very bad.

Scowl did not sound like he was very nice at all!

The Autobots knew they needed to find Scowl before he joined up with his gang.

Grimlock was sorry about what he had done. "I promise I won't let you down again," he told Bumblebee.

"OK," said Bumblebee. "The important thing is that you help make it right."

The Autobots transformed into cars. "Time to wreck and roll!" Bumblebee cried.

## Chapter Five

# TRAITOR!

When they reached the woods, the Autobots changed back into robots. They marched through the trees, searching for Scowl.

"I still don't think Scowl is a bad bot," Grimlock told the others. He really couldn't believe that his new friend was as bad as everyone thought he was.

Grimlock told Bumblebee that Scowl could stop being bad.

After all, Grimlock had changed. "I could take him under my claw," said Grimlock, "and show him how to be good."

Bumblebee and the other Autobots weren't convinced.

"He is my friend!" said Grimlock. "He promised not to hurt anyone."

Suddenly, someone leaped out of the trees and attacked Grimlock. It was Scowl!

"Scowl, you promised that you would not hurt anyone," Grimlock said.

Scowl laughed meanly. "I lied, you silly Dinobot! I will do whatever I want!"

Grimlock felt sad. Scowl WAS bad, after all!

Scowl tried to smash Grimlock with his tail. Then he picked up a tree and threw it on top of the Autobots.

As Grimlock lifted the tree off his team, Scowl ran off through the woods. The bad Dinobot was really angry!

## Chapter Six

# STATION SMASH-UP

The Autobots chased after Scowl and finally caught up with him at the train station. Scowl smashed his spiky tail into the side of a bus. *CRUNCH!* Then he lifted it up high and threw it at the Autobots!

Scowl climbed up on to the railway bridge. He wanted to smash it. The Autobots jumped up and blocked his way.

"You are under arrest," Bumblebee said. "We can't let you wreck this place – humans use it every day."

But the Dinobot just laughed. "They won't be using it any more!"

Scowl shot up into the air then crashed down on to the railway bridge. *CRAAAAACK!* The bridge started to break!

Grimlock tried to talk to Scowl. "Please stop," he told the other Dinobot. "You could use your smashing to do good.

Doesn't that sound great?"

"That sounds boring," sneered Scowl. "I will smash whatever I want and I'm not stopping. You can't make me!"

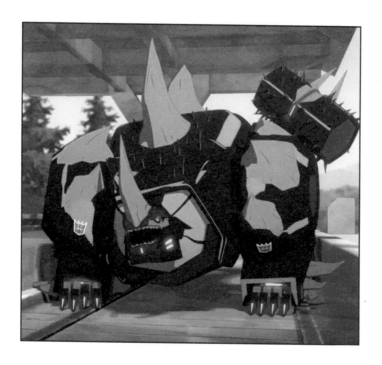

Grimlock and Scowl started
to fight. They locked tails and
tried to push each other off
the platform. The bad Dinobot
whacked Grimlock with his tail.
*SLAM!* Grimlock hit him back.

"You are not a real Dinobot!"
Scowl jeered.

"I AM a Dinobot!" roared Grimlock. He charged at Scowl.

"Well, you don't act like one," sneered Scowl.

Grimlock bashed Scowl so hard he flew out of the train station.

In the distance, a whistle blew. "Quick, we need to fix the bridge," Bumblebee ordered the other Autobots. "There's a train coming!"

Part Three:
THE LAST BATTLE

# Chapter Seven

## SPA DAY

The Autobots stood under the bridge, holding up big pieces of the track. But it was no use. The bridge was too badly damaged to be fixed.

The Autobots heard an announcement. "The last train is now arriving." They needed to act fast!

Bumblebee had an idea. "Knock it all down!" he said.

*SMASH! CRASH!* The robots pounded the bridge with their fists and the rest of the track crashed to the ground. Soon, the whole bridge was destroyed.

"Now we need to make a new bridge," said Strongarm.

Grimlock and all the Autobots stood together in a line and raised their arms up as high as they could. The Autobots made a new bridge – out of themselves!

As the speeding train raced towards them, the Autobots caught it. The train was heavy, but the Autobots were strong!

The train and all the passengers were safe, but Scowl had escaped …

The Autobots fixed the bridge properly, then followed Scowl's trail of destruction. They arrived at a peaceful spa. There were lots of people in white bathrobes and towels, relaxing by the swimming pool. But the spa was not very calm any more.

"Eek!" shrieked the people, catching sight of the huge brown Dinobot.

"That's enough, Scowl!" said Bumblebee. But Scowl ignored Bumblebee. He chased the people inside the spa.

"Let's split up," Bumblebee ordered the Autobots. "Don't let Scowl get away!"

## Chapter Eight

# A CHANGE OF HEART

Drift and his two students searched the shower room. They tried to be quiet, but Scowl was even quieter. He crept up behind them and smashed them with his tail!

Grimlock was looking for Scowl in the lobby. He saw a fountain made out of a huge stone ball, but he didn't see the Dinobot anywhere.

"Come out here now, Scowl," he called out, "or you will regret it."

Scowl charged around the corner, his horn lowered. He tackled Grimlock to the ground with a loud *THUMP*.

Nearby, a group of people were sitting with their eyes closed. They were so calm they didn't even realise that there was a Dinobot attacking the spa!

Scowl smashed the pillars holding up the roof. The roof started tumbling down. It was going to crush the humans!

Grimlock raced over and caught all the pieces of roof just in time. As he struggled to hold the heavy pieces, Scowl just laughed at him meanly.

"You are an Autobot, Grimlock,"
he said, "which means you are
not a Dinobot any more."

Grimlock didn't reply. Instead
he threw the pieces of roof
at Scowl! Scowl ducked.

Snarling and growling, the two Dinobots battled each other again. They charged at each other over and over, smashing with their tails and biting with their sharp jaws.

Scowl gave a big roar and threw Grimlock on the floor.

"OK, OK," said Grimlock. "You're right. It's a lot easier and more fun to smash up whatever I want instead of being told what to do by an Autobot."

Grimlock was going to be bad, just like Scowl!

## Chapter Nine

# IT'S A KNOCKOUT

"That's more like it," Scowl laughed. "I knew you'd come around, big guy! Now give me a tail-five."

Grimlock got back to his feet. He turned around, but he didn't give Scowl a tail-five. Instead, he whacked the stone fountain with his tail. The huge stone ball flew into the air and hit Scowl. The bad Dinobot fell to the floor.

Grimlock had only been pretending! He would NEVER stop fighting – not when a Decepticon was trying to hurt people.

"Just because something is more fun doesn't make it right," he told Scowl.

"Nice capture, Grim," said Strongarm, as the other Autobots came to arrest Scowl.

"I know you just wanted to help Scowl," Bumblebee told Grimlock.

Grimlock hadn't managed to change Scowl. But he had learned an important lesson. "You don't have to do something bad just because your friends think it is cool," he said.

"When did you get so smart?" Bumblebee said, smiling at Grimlock.

Looking around at Sideswipe, Strongarm, Bee and the others, Grimlock suddenly realised something. He didn't need a friend who was a Dinobot.

The Autobots were his friends and they would never let him down. Grimlock smiled. Having good friends was even better than smashing things!

The End

# WELL DONE!

You've finished this adventure!

# Have you read the other exciting Transformers Early Readers?

EARLY READER

TRANSFORMERS ROBOTS IN DISGUISE
BUMBLEBEE THE BOSS

EARLY READER

TRANSFORMERS ROBOTS IN DISGUISE
SIDESWIPE'S BRAVE PLAN